Robert Louis Stevenson & Robert Hunter

THE LAND OF NOD

FLYING EYE BOOKS

London-New York

From breakfast on through all the day

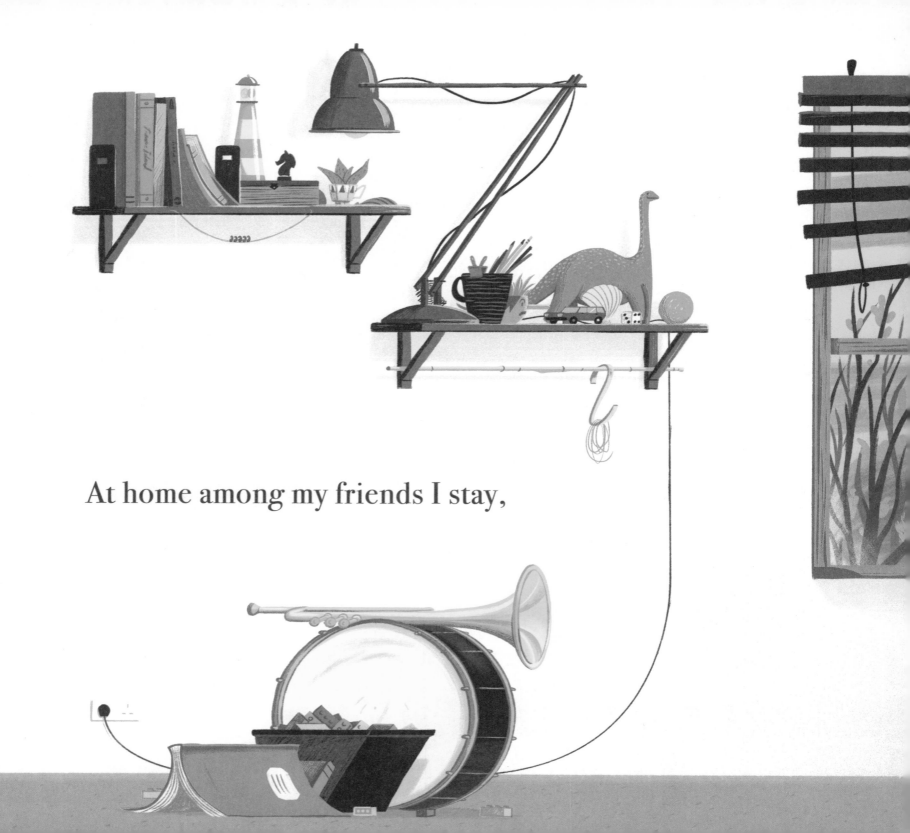

At home among my friends I stay,

But every night I go abroad

Afar into the land of Nod.

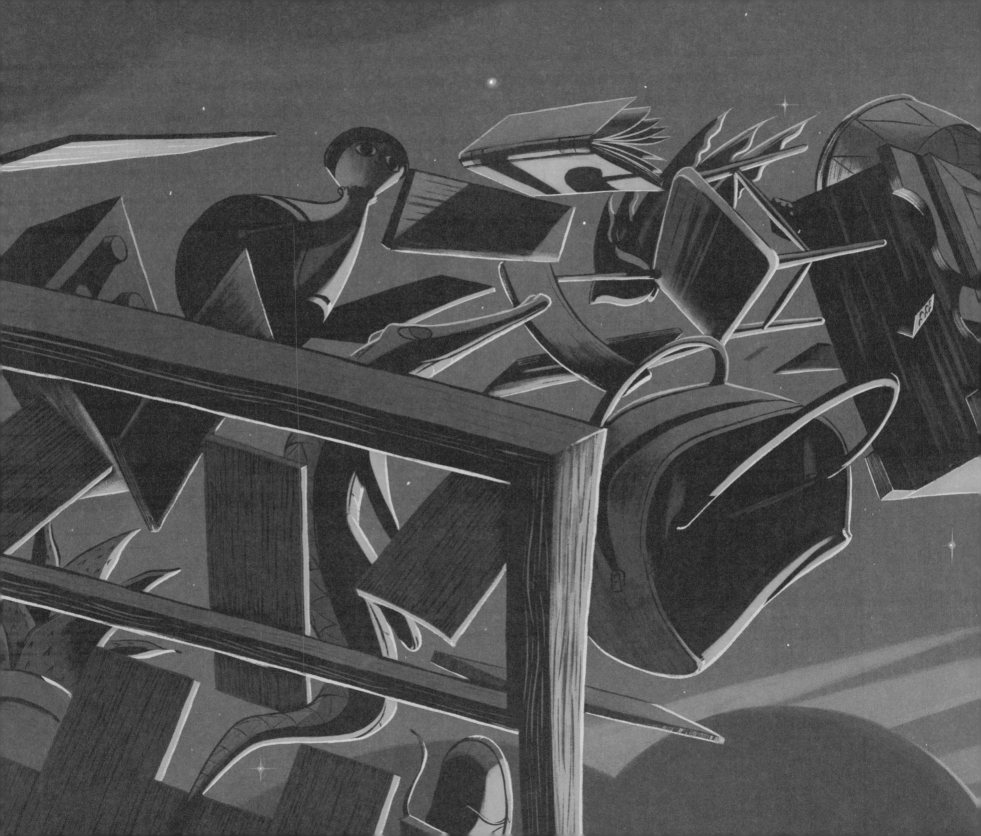

All by myself I have to go,

With none to tell me what to do —

All alone beside the streams

And up the mountain-sides of dreams.

The strangest things are there for me,

Both things to eat and things to see,

And many frightening sights abroad

Till morning in the land of Nod.

Try as I like to find the way,

I never can get back by day,

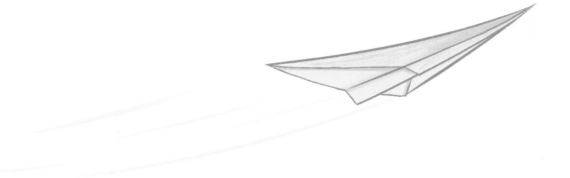

Nor can remember plain and clear

The curious music that I hear.

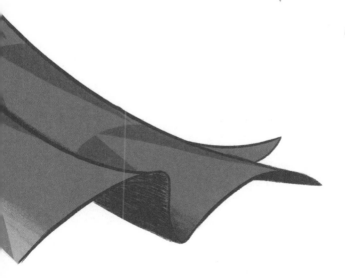